For Nikki &
Jess Illes

the original
Panda Big &
Panda Small!

I'd like to thank Naia, for giving her time
to make this story end up as a rhyme.

First published in Great Britain in 1998
by Dorling Kindersley Limited,
9 Henrietta Street, London WC2E 8PS

Copyright © 1998 Jane Cabrera
The author and illustrator's moral rights have been asserted.

Visit us on the World Wide Web at http://www.dk.com

A CIP catalogue record for this book is available from the British Library.

ISBN 0 7513 7079 7 (Hardback)
ISBN 0 7513 7183 1 (Paperback)

Colour reproduction by Dot Gradations, UK
Printed in Hong Kong by Wing King Tong

Help Save the Panda

There are ONLY between 1000 and
2000 pandas left in the wild in
China. They need our help.
For information contact:

World Wide Fund for Nature
Panda House
Weyside Park
Godalming
Surrey GU7 1XR
Telephone 01483 426444

Panda Big and Panda Small

Jane Cabrera

Panda Big and Panda Small

do not like the

same things at all.

Panda Big likes to be **asleep** at the beginning of the day.

Panda Small is wide **awake** and wants to go and play!

Panda Big
likes to sit and
think at the
bottom
of these trees.

Panda Small is at the **top** peeping through the leaves.

Panda Big likes to have her eyes **open** to watch the insects fly.

Panda Small has hers tight **shut** when these come dropping by!

Panda Big
likes to eat
in front of
the bamboo.

Panda Small is there
behind playing peekaboo.

Panda Big likes to be **still** when lying on the ground.

tickle tickle

Panda Small just can't help **moving** noisily around.

Panda Big
likes to swing slowly
on the rope that's **long**.

Panda Small is on the one that's **short**. I hope she's hanging on!

Panda Big likes to stay **out** of the water, standing in the sun.

Panda Small has fallen **in** and thinks it's such good fun.

But when **Panda Big** and
Panda Small are **near** and

far

it makes them rather sad.

And then they know there's just one

thing that makes them **both** feel glad . . .

Being
together.

Now that's better.

Other Toddler Books to collect -

I'M TOO BUSY by Helen Stephens

CATERPILLAR'S WISH by Mary Murphy

BABY LOVES by Michael Lawrence, Illustrated by Adrian Reynolds

THE PIG WHO WISHED by Joyce Dunbar, Illustrated by Selina Young